LITTLE WOLF

Peter Donnelly

For my sister Suzanne, with love x
P.D.

HODDER CHILDREN'S BOOKS

First published in Great Britain in 2023
by Hodder and Stoughton

1 3 5 7 9 10 8 6 4 2

© Hodder & Stoughton Limited, 2023
Text and illustrations by Peter Donnelly

A CIP catalogue record for this book is available from the British Library.

HB ISBN: 978 1 44496 770 8
PB ISBN: 978 1 44496 772 2

Printed and bound in China

MIX
Paper from
responsible sources
FSC® C104740
FSC
www.fsc.org

Hodder Children's Books
An imprint of Hachette Children's Group
Part of Hodder and Stoughton Limited
Carmelite House, 50 Victoria Embankment, London, EC4Y 0DZ

An Hachette UK Company
www.hachette.co.uk
www.hachettechildrens.co.uk

Hodder
Children's
Books

LITTLE WOLF

Peter Donnelly

Little Wolf lived in a deep valley, surrounded by pine forests and rocky mountains.

Every day was an adventure for Little Wolf and his brother and sisters.

Together they raced through the forest, tumbled in the mud and splashed across bubbling streams.

And, each night, the pups curled up in their cosy den, listening to Big Wolf's tales of long ago.

One day, Big Wolf made an important announcement.

"Gather round, pups. Very soon, all the wolves in this valley will come together for the Howling Ceremony. The moon will be bright. The crowds will be huge! And on that night, each of you must howl your very best howl to prove that you are ready to join the pack."

The pups jumped up, eager to get started.

"My howl will be the best in the whole valley," said one pup.

"Mine will be the loudest," cried another.

But Little Wolf was worried.
He didn't feel brave enough to
howl in front of a great big crowd.

Quietly, he slipped into the forest.
Then he took a deep breath and tried to howl.

But all he could manage was a tiny . . .

"EEEKKK!"

Little Wolf heard a rustling sound in the bushes . . .

"Hey, little squeak!" the other pups giggled.

"Now, now pups," said Big Wolf, appearing through the trees.
"That's no way to treat your little brother. Scatter back to your den!
Don't worry, Little Wolf," he smiled. "Take your time and practise."

The next morning, Little Wolf marched off into the forest with his head held high. "*Today* I am going to howl. I know it, I really do!"

Little Wolf found his favourite spot
in the woods. He sat up straight
and took a deep breath but all
that came out was an . . .

"EEEKKK!"

"It's no good," sighed Little Wolf.
"I just can't do it."

Spring turned to summer and the Howling Ceremony drew closer.

With each passing day, Little Wolf's brother's and sisters' barks and growls grew louder and stronger.

But Little Wolf could still only manage a squeak. "I'm not a real wolf," he said sadly. "I'll *never* be a real wolf without a howl."

"Don't worry," Big Wolf said gently. "You will find your own special voice when the time is right."

At last, the night of the ceremony arrived.
A supermoon lit up the valley as a huge, excited
crowd gathered at Howling Rock.

"My pups have grown strong," said Big Wolf.
"The time has come for them to show that they
are ready to join our wolf pack."

EEEEKK!"

Silence filled Howling Rock.

"I'll never be able to join the wolf pack," said Little Wolf sadly.

"It's OK," whispered Big Wolf. "You just need to howl in your own way. Try again, but this time from your heart."

Little Wolf looked out across the valley.
The treetops glistened beneath the silver moon.
The snowy mountain peaks shimmered in the moonlight.

He closed his eyes tightly, took a
deep breath and . . .

LA-LA-LAAAAAA!"

Out came the sweetest, most wonderful

song the wolf pack had ever heard!

"Wow! Little Wolf, you really do have the most
beautiful voice," cried his brother and sisters in amazement.

"Well done, my little wolf," smiled Big Wolf proudly. "You have found
your true voice in your own special way. Welcome to our pack."

Little Wolf looked out at the cheering crowds and smiled.
"My song is different, and that's what makes it special.
That's what makes ME special."

And now, on nights when the
supermoon lights up the sky, you might just
hear Little Wolf singing his song in the distance –
a song of happiness and freedom that echoes
from the mountain-tops.

"LA-LA-LA-LA-LAAAAAA!!!"